7/23

Feeling Grateful

How to add more goodness to your gladness

———————

Written by Kobi Yamada
Illustrated by Charles Santoso

Gratitude isn't just something you have, it's something you learn and develop. It's a life skill. You can grow your capacity for gratefulness. You can cultivate your ability to pause, to look around, to be surprised and delighted by the world around you. When you slow down, you can better honor and feel the gift of each moment and the opportunity that comes with it.

Life is a gift. And it is for you.

The best things in life often aren't things at all. They are experiences lived, emotions felt, and connections made. These are the things that sparkle in our memory. And it is when we are feeling grateful that we can perform our most beautiful acts and appreciate our most treasured moments.

Look closely. The extraordinary is hidden in the ordinary.
It is in the appreciation of something that we really begin to see it.

Think of what makes you smile. A hug from a friend.
An act of compassion. Contagious laughter. A blooming flower.
So many of life's delights are available to you.

Be present for your life. Keep hold of small joys. You can miss *what is* while regretting *what could have been* or worrying about *what could be*.

Love freely, openly, abundantly.
The more love you share, the more love you have.

Simplify. Not much is needed for happiness.

Share your gifts and help others to unwrap their own.

None of us make it through life alone.
Take time to pause and reflect on those
who have helped you along the way.

We all need to encourage each other's growth.
Never underestimate the power of a kind word.
There's always a way to give it, say it, do it with heart.

Look for what you admire and share a
sincere compliment. Everyone appreciates
being appreciated.

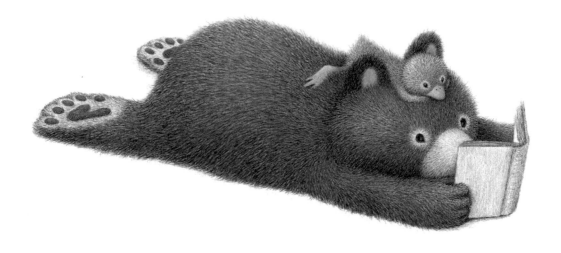

Be the reason someone believes in the goodness of people. Every kind thing you say or do for another becomes a part of them, and you.

Reach out, be willing, welcome connection.
What an honor it is to be counted on. What a privilege
it is to be thought of. The most meaningful things in life
are meant to be shared: stories, memories, love.

Be there for others. Good people help good people to be good people.

If you are disappointed that you didn't get what you wanted, take heart. And consider all the times you didn't get what you *didn't* want.

Be proud of your resiliency. Give yourself credit for making it through the tough times when it felt like you might not.

Talk to yourself in a way that is kind
and nurturing, because you are listening.

Admire the beauty and value of others without questioning your own.

Look for a need. Seek out a problem.
Give back in a way that is meaningful to you. Be the
difference that changes something for the better.

Feel the ground, smell the air, touch the light, drink the sky.
You are not just a part of nature, nature is a part of you.

Have adventures. Go places.
Seek out as many of the world's
wonders that you possibly can.

Love with everything you are
because love deserves nothing less.

Ask questions worthy of your attention.
What makes you happy? How will you
help another? What do you love most about
being alive? What are you grateful for?

This day will never happen again. Everything
is a once-in-a-lifetime experience. Give thanks
in this moment. And this moment. And this moment.
And all your moments going forward.

Written by: Kobi Yamada

Illustrated by: Charles Santoso

Edited by: Kristin Eade

Art Directed by: Justine Edge

Library of Congress Control Number: 2021944305 | ISBN: 978-1-970147-73-5

3rd printing. Printed in China with soy inks on FSC®-Mix certified paper.

Create meaningful moments with gifts that inspire.

CONNECT WITH US

live-inspired.com | sayhello@compendiuminc.com

   @compendiumliveinspired
#compendiumliveinspired